DR XARGLE'S
BOOK OF
EARTH TIGGERS

For Wilbur, Fatty and Sue

A Red Fox Book

Published by Random House Children's Books
20 Vauxhall Bridge Road, London SW1V 2SA

A division of Random House UK Ltd
London Melbourne Sydney Auckland
Johannesburg and agencies throughout the world

First published by Andersen Press Ltd 1990

This edition Red Fox 1992

7 9 10 8 6

Text copyright © Jeanne Willis 1990
Illustrations © copyright Tony Ross 1990

The rights of Jeanne Willis and Tony Ross to be identified as the
author and illustrator of this work have been asserted by them
in accordance with the Copyright, Designs and Patents Act, 1988.

Printed in Hong Kong

RANDOM HOUSE UK Limited Reg. No. 954009

ISBN 0 09 988140 3

DR XARGLE'S BOOK OF EARTH TIGGERS

Translated into Human by Jeanne Willis
Pictures by Tony Ross

RED FOX

Good morning, class.

Today we are going to learn about Earth Tiggers. Earth Tiggers are made of furry material. This does up underneath with pink buttons.

They are available in Patterned or Plain.

Press them in the middle to find the squeaker.

Earth Tiggers grow sharp thorns.
These they use to carve objects made of wood.

Or to climb steep Earthlets.

Earth Tiggers like gardening. They dig a hole and
plant a stinkpod. This never grows.

During the rainy season, stinkpods may be planted
in any container found in the earthdwelling.

Earth Tiggers like breakfast at 5 a.m. Precisely.
They massage the pyjamas of the sleeping Earthlet.
Then they sit on his nostrils.

Earth Tiggers eat meatblob.

This they collect on their many antennae to save for later.

A healthy Earth Tigger also needs cowjuice, tandoori cluck bird, muckworm and old green gibble in dustbin gravy.

Earth Tiggers can hear a parcel of pigrolls being opened five earth miles away.

They cannot hear an Earthlet shouting "Tiddles!" in the next garden.

Earth Tiggers hate the Earth Hound.
They fold in half and puff air into their waggler.
Then they go into orbit with a hiss and a crackle.

In a glass capsule full of stones and vegetables lives
the sparkly, golden fishstick.

This the Earth Tigger likes. He puts his mitten into the water and mixes the fishstick all about.

Earth Tiggers like to sing loudly in the moonlight with their friends. The Earthling hurls items of footwear all around.

Earth Tiggers sometimes put a hairy pudding on the stairs. The Earthling is made to step on this with no socks on.

Repeat this phrase after me:
"Whoops, I have slipped on a furball and broken both my legs."

Sometimes the Earth Tigger gets torn and must be taken to the menders. First he must be caught and wrapped in cardboard and string. The Earthlet sticks himself back together with pink paper.

When Earth Tiggers are born, the Earthlet gives them a bed made from knitted twigs and a bag of birdfluff. This the Tiggerlets hate.

They go to sleep in the headdress of the Earthling.

Dear me, is that the time?
Put on your disguises and get into the spaceship quickly.
We're going to Planet Earth to stroke Tiggerlets.

We'll be landing in India at dinnertime.

Some
bestselling Red Fox
picture books

THE BIG ALFIE AND ANNIE ROSE STORYBOOK
by Shirley Hughes
OLD BEAR
by Jane Hissey
OI! GET OFF OUR TRAIN
by John Burningham
DON'T DO THAT!
by Tony Ross
NOT NOW, BERNARD
by David McKee
ALL JOIN IN
by Quentin Blake
THE WHALES' SONG
by Gary Blythe and Dyan Sheldon
JESUS' CHRISTMAS PARTY
by Nicholas Allan
THE PATCHWORK CAT
by Nicola Bayley and William Mayne

WILLY AND HUGH
by Anthony Browne
THE WINTER HEDGEHOG
by Ann and Reg Cartwright
A DARK, DARK TALE
by Ruth Brown
HARRY, THE DIRTY DOG
by Gene Zion and Margaret Bloy Graham
DR XARGLE'S BOOK OF EARTHLETS
by Jeanne Willis and Tony Ross
WHERE'S THE BABY?
by Pat Hutchins